I0633771

Hammerite
Spider

Peter Plant

chipmunkapublishing
the mental health publisher

Published by

Chipmunkapublishing

PO Box 6872

Brentwood

Essex CM13 1ZT

United Kingdom

http://www.chipmunkapublishing.com

Copyright © Peter Plant 2012

Edited by Tom Parmiter

ISBN 978-1-84991-797-1

Chipmunkapublishing gratefully acknowledge the support of Arts Council England.

Snake pit

Onto wired panes

Fixed in twin skins

Spat schizophrenic March.

From hazy blue unwanted rooms

Smoke-screened Rattlers hiss -

Popped and shed patsies scaled

And scared.

Mongoose nurse's dish

Prescriptive hits in some

Wits pit of fancy.

For you Bro

I fell from the skies mother, into your arms

So warm; so warm.

Free of charge or favour on a night

So cold; so cold.

But for you my brother:-

A mangy dog in a doorway

To hold; to hold.

Sand/cement/mothwing

And the Lord said: *'what kind of a house will you build for me?'*

It was in the cash only store that Joey last saw the Great Moths fluttering up from the line of tills out of the spent purses, ears of the deaf, bursting free from the teat's of dummies spilled onto the breasts of sleeping babies growing as they rose till their wings spanned 2 feet or more. Great powdery Angels laying bare their motifs, longing to be seen, longing to be heard becoming thunderous in the roof-space, drumming; clanking off the large section air conditioning ducts threshing their wings on steel hangers holding up the galvanized cable trays. Opening up old wounds it seemed and fusing all unnatural light so that the store became veiled in a spectral glow pulsating from their ethereal bodies. The light made hazy by dust and moth-wing.

Joey wasn't fazed or surprised by any of it really. He'd been expecting them, or something like. He knew he couldn't be so grimly disassembled without experiencing some form of visitation. Not long out of hospital after treatment for bipolar depression with the usual zap'n'pill'n'wrist-rubber bling he'd come out too early, but just didn't have the stomach for it anymore. This coupled with the realisation that he was on the most God-awful shit hole of a mental health ward he'd ever been on. He'd had to go in though - or risk being sectioned. World weary; broken, always fighting drug dependency anyway - he wanted to walk new roads lain, pitched up in their perfection; not ones bearing the scars every few hundred yards for service pipes, sunken drains; or roam the woods like a charcoal burner crunching on acorns - and for a long time anti-psychiatry. He'd had to convince the shrink though. His thinking was to make sure his eyes were right. Maintain eye contact and smile. He'd noticed over the decades that they concentrate on the eyes, must be part of the training he figured. Anyway, he got out.

Watching the Great Moths, Joey had trailed behind his wife who was now further on up the fruit and veg aisle. With one hand on the shopping trolley she reached out the other for a cabbage. Time paused for Joey as he watched. The tatty fleece she was wearing now covered in the luminous fallout from above gave her the look of a sandstone statue holding the rail of a chariot pointing to freedom and the Promised Land. The queen of poverty he thought. Boudicca of the cheap beans 'n'veg.

How had it come to this...?

Adam looked down on Joey through the mists of his own making with a heart heavy like a compassionate Nazi compelled to mute his sadness at the struggles of man from atop a gantry at a forced labour camp. His young friend now grey and stooped. Where was the fit looking lad he'd come to love and respect from 35 years previous with his long mousey hair sporting a curious white patch to the right side of his head formed by a caustic reaction from the compo in the hod he carried? His wit as cauterised as his hair. Adam had always refused to believe that the muck in the hod had whitened his hair - he reckoned he carried saints. He longed to talk to him. To ask him why he thought he didn't make it. To tell him how he'd called out for him again but knew he couldn't hear. To tell him he never wanted to break his parent's hearts or spirit.

Joey sat on the last stack of bricks he'd loaded out and stripped to the waist. His tee-shirt reeked with the pungency of leaking ale and sweat and he trembled in the heat like a half-starved dog edging closer to a bigger dog's bone. Should be a nice place to work this; in the Warwickshire countryside, extending a remote detached house skirted by woodland. He left his perch long enough to soak himself head to foot with the hosepipe filling the water but then sat back down. Could be a good place to die. The wind picked up and the mania in the trees became oppressive. He checked over his work; neatly stacked bricks, engineers and blues to take the build to damp-proof level interspersed with spot boards for the compo, all easy reach for the brickies'. He knew his job, he was good at it.

The child appeared; as he did every day. Joey saw in his eyes something that he had lost; the child something he had gained. He disappeared. The trees were mad with rustle. Joey crossed the paddock to offer himself up to the timber wolves that had pursued him relentlessly for months frothing and snarling at the edge of the wood. For the first time in his life he was ready to die.

Big Gerry had been unloading cement from his pick-up truck at the back of the house when the child appeared. He reached out and took Gerry's huge dried-out-cowpat-for-a-hand and led him round the house to find Joey staring at trees. The child disappeared. Gerry walked over to Joey.

'What's up kid?'

Joey was too choked up to speak - and hod carriers just weren't meant to cry.

Gerry had known something had been troubling Joey for months, and as he pulled off the driveway to take him home and looked over at his meticulous preparation he knew Joey wouldn't be involved in the build. It would be left to others to piece it all together. For a man thought of as being as impervious as a blue brick when trying to absorb anything or one a bit queer nothing was dug for by Gerry on the way home. Or explanation expected from Joey. They were to work together many more times.

Joey took his first peek inside a Columbian billionaires wallet in '75 aged 23. He shook into that particular nuthouse like a shell-shock victim nodding at everyone and no-one.

'Come to dry out?'

A numpty male 'nurse' spoke from the mental darkness that was his station; through the visible darkness of his tinted bins. Joey was seriously ill, but not blind.

The first bricks went down.

He spent the first week pretty much alone in a single room off the main corridor medicated and injected in alternate buttocks every day to help combat the effects of alcoholism and getting used to the smells of stale smoke and misery. The liqueur he'd been shelling out for for the last 5 years to stave off panic and anxiety was firing duds. He was rock bottom. Majorly depressed. Mogadon helped him sleep through the shrieks and banshee wails in dimly-lit dreams. All the pills he took made him sleepy. They must know what they're doing he thought. He knew depression didn't like to sleep. Maybe if they kept forcing sleep onto it it would get pissed off and leave him out of boredom. Joey only remembered the names of two drugs from that first visit - mogadon (which among others he was on) and largactil - the one that all the major players seemed to be on. Sleep and madness; madness asleep.

To the tearless eye he looked way out of place. Tanned, wash-boarded; he looked like he'd been working out all summer on a tropical beach, more a boxer than a wreck; but a wreck he was. The shell of a Maserati in a back street car-body repair shop; a polished dovetailed toolbox loaded with blunt tools.

He studied his hands a lot - brick hard and calloused - and tried to soften them up with snot and tears. He didn't deserve hands as such, or his taut bull terrier like body. It just didn't add up. His was a body that carried great weight – what was going off in his head?

So here was Joey: hard and soft, hot or cold. A curious mix of brick-dust and blancmange with a heart like the summer sun in a cumulous sky; full-on or half-hidden.

Joey began to walk the corridors after about a week. Long and echoey. The sounds bounced round his head like a night jungle. The human imagery like a carboniferous jungle. Strange and sweaty. Too hot. He noticed the sash windows locked off at 6 inches and all the glass was wired plate to keep the fists in. He reckoned he could punch one out; he tried to on his next visit. He was in a Lowry painting: men shuffling along in ill-fitting slippers; flannelette world; knobs and bogies hanging out. Women in the same state of preventable slovenliness; flannelette world. The whole encapsulated by the Mongol (term still in use in the seventies) haircuts - what the fuck's with the hair? For fuck sake get a decent barber in - they're not on Lindisfarne writing the Anglo-Saxon fuckin' chronicles! He got angry pretty quick.

More muck! More muck!

He was troubled by a middle aged woman who took a shine to him. Everywhere he went she followed taking items of clothing off. She wanted him to fuck her. Joey was too young and fussy; he wasn't up for it. He tried to fend her off as best he could. The staff were pretty much anonymous most of the time and the situation became a pain. He did his best to keep out of her way but ended up shutting himself away. Joey was puzzled when, a couple of weeks later, the same woman sat quietly in the corner of the lounge, a different woman, not wanting anything from him; not even recognising him.

One bad day Joey sat in the lounge trying to read a magazine that he picked up off one of the coffee tables. He was too low; his concentration wasn't good enough, so he began watching a girl, probably in her late teens sitting opposite on a tatty brown leather armchair rocking back and forth. After a series of rocks she would stop, look to the heavens, and mime a scream. The tendons in her neck stuck out but no sound. What's going on he thought? Was she orgasmic or forcing a crap? The flannelette robe had parted down the middle exposing her nightie. She must be on one of those section orders he'd heard about. He started to count the rocks between the stops for whatever the stopped rocks clocked up in her head to see if they formed a series. Sometimes ten, sometimes twelve, sometimes eight. No, there was no pattern. He did notice though that the rocking caused her nightie to inch its way up her thighs. He'd lost his thread; it became unclear what revelation he was seeking: the cause and cure of her deranged anguish or what colour her knickers would be that were about to make an appearance. He fancied a plate of salted whelks. He fancied dying. He cried that night.

There was another woman on the ward that moved Joey; late twenties, with a horrendous scar round her neck almost from ear to ear. He overheard someone say that she'd cut her own throat. At visiting time one day he noticed her with a visitor sat on a stool holding her hand and whispering softly to her. She had to slowly turn her shoulders with her head to look round in case her head fell off. What the fuck-of-a-blade did she use he thought? It looked like she'd taken a chainsaw to it. The livid scar jagged its way round her throat like the relieved grimace of a masochist. He wanted to talk to her but felt verbally inarticulate; kiss her throat maybe.

These and other haunting images that would scare a ghost shitless would stay with Joey always.

He wasn't prepared for all this. Why wasn't he prepared for all this? They'd banned the freak show in the travelling fairs when he was a kid - the twins in pickled jars.

These brickies were fast.

Joey was always 'lucky'. He fumbled about in the foulest pits with the best of them but was like a monkey on a ladder. Must be his job, maybe he was a boxer. He was never down there for years like some of the poor sods and after seven or eight weeks of E.C.T. and medication Joey's spirit began to tap him on the shoulder along with an ever developing sardonic humour. Some days he felt enlightened enough to feel like a shepherd overseeing his flock; like he'd been visited by the Angel Gabriel who'd told him to spread the word that all will be okay - eventually. He named his flock. Among whom was Largactil. A lad no older than Joey who he liked to watch when the drug trolley moved in. Largactil trod water when taking his syrup like a kid forcing down milk of magnesia. They had to be on his case at medico time because he just daint like the stuff! Or the effects. Joey knew fuck-all about the serious shit these people were on but he guessed enough to reckon whatever it was made valium seem like a pack of smarties. He'd neck it down like someone who hated whiskey but drank it anyway - like Joey - then shuffle away chuntering to himself. Short steps. The Largactil shuffle they called it.

Then there was Willow. A huge Rastafarian brought to the ward by two coppers. His sweeping dreadlocks reminded Joey of the great tree by his favourite peg on the river. Willow got to like Joey, he thought him an 'umble marn'. Probably because he supplied him with regular roll-ups. Molly was a puzzle. A well-built man with broad shoulders and a heavy beard shadow always decked out in a bright red dress far too small for him. He passed off as a woman as convincingly as Dolly Parton would an Olympic weightlifter.

Although on good days Joey felt a bit of a fraud being amongst such serious lunatics - this place was once a shelter for 'tramps, lunatics, paupers, imbeciles and idiots'; terms used in the 19th century with distinctive definitions- he never felt out of place. He belonged with these people and his natural empathetic nature flourished. He became a bewildered idolater. Bent with the pain of their sufferings, bent double with the hilarity of some of the antics and conversations. A child at a pantomime:

Largactil- I'm fuckin' mad I am!

Joey- Oh no you're not!

Shrink- Oh yes he is!

Largactil- Where's the God I was just talking to?

Joey- He's behind you!

Shrink- Oh no he isn't!

On one of the mornings when the chancer laid his bricks Joey was sharing a roll-up with Willow in the lounge. Willow played a badly tuned guitar while singing 'I Shot the Sheriff'. The big man fiddled with the tuning keys but the sound got worse. Joey tended to laugh when edgy or trying not to laugh but something was telling him not to because the great man knew exactly what he was doing. And Willow was nineteen stone of unpredictable whatever-he-was. For all Joey knew he may well have shot the sheriff.

Any thought of laughter went down the pan when Joey met the cowboy. One of the main shrinks' undershrinks, so shrunken in his obnoxious ignorance that Joey never forgot or forgave. He blasted Joey for even being there; asking him why he wasn't out there working. The place wasn't a half-way house for benefit scroungers. This pretty much shattered Joey. A 23-year-old thinking he was going mad. One of Joey's proudest achievements in later life was his employment record - well over 90% of his working life spent in employment - not bad for a mentally ill shyster.

Joey withdrew into himself again and became a concern. One of the nurses tried to explain to Joey that the thousand bricks a day man was always like that. It was just his way! Joey went backwards and after a time was seen by another shrink. More affable. He listened to what he had to say as a young wife would to her husband's groveling apology after taking her first battering. He suggested to Joey that he might benefit from being on the new group therapy unit. Apparently the residents were all about his age and were struggling with problems that were more emotional or neurotic than psychotic. Joey hadn't a clue what neurotic meant - he didn't know what any of it meant - he'd not been told anything other than that he was experiencing a total breakdown of confidence. This was all as clear as mud to Joey. All he knew was that he'd become shit scared of life and he hadn't always been shit scared of life; in fact there were times he felt almost bear-like in confidence. He'd took to drinking shed loads of alcohol straight out of bed which temporarily made him not shit scared of life but when it wore off he became even shittier scared of life and the shittier scared he became the more depressed he became. But of course Joey was young and unable to explain things succinctly! Get rid of the panic, the alcohol shielding the panic and he would be as sound as the Flemish bond walling that held up this place.

Always conscious of the anxiety levels that were to render him speechless when in formal settings, he moved onto the unit as inconspicuously as he could. Why had he crawled down a funneled opening like a lobster? He'd put himself into the type of situation that had bought him here in the first place. He'd have to sit in on meetings every morning and try to control the panic that was plaguing his life to such an extent that suicide had become an option. Maybe that's what he needed to do - put himself into these positions - purge it out. Now no more a notion than conviction he was in the right place, he set about formulating a plan as how to dodge the verbal bullets that were bound to shoot his way at his first meeting. Would they smell liqueur he thought? Bound to. His only hope would be if they picked out another member of the group first to give his heart time to run out of bounce like a rubber ball losing its battle against gravity. Fuck all of this, fuck it all.

Joey managed that first meeting somehow. He got away with introducing himself then clammed up. Luckily something had gone on the day before that had created interest and he was ignored for the rest of the meeting.

He got to know the lads first: Paul was an introvert with a real hang-up about having red hair. He thought people might think him Irish. Joey suggested that people might think him Scottish but that didn't ease his burden. He lay on the bed most of the day with head phones on listening to Leonard Cohen, Joni Mitchell and other poet-cum-folk-singy artists. Joey never asked what was wrong with him; he never asked what was wrong with anyone on that first visit because he understood very little about mental illness. As far as he could make out there were those obviously off the scale and ununderstandable and those who seemed okay like him but clearly didn't have all their oars in the water neurotically, emotionally, or whatever elsely.

Jake was a nasty bastard; an original late sixties ex skinhead type, out of place, a cuckoo in a nest of feeble chicks who liked nothing better than to try and fuck them out over the edge; particularly the more sensitive souls. He left Joey alone; his physical make-up and aura of volatility made him too high risk. Joey walked into the dorm one night to catch Jake singing 'Billy McGinty's goat' to Paul who was really strung out. As said, a nasty bastard.

Adam was a real problem for Joey. When his hod was full and he could bear no more weight he did his head in with his complete social ineptitude. When he'd stacked out his load and was burden free he wanted to take him under his wing and look out for him. Joey felt like some sort of a sage when in his company and spent hours making him laugh, encouraging him. Adam liked his street savvy and drunken tales. He wished he could be like him. Joey watched him often while he slept, always sensing the fragility beneath the skin of the 21-year-old social misfit.

Adam was from a good background, not rich but flush enough for him to own an Alpha Romeo and lash out £500 on a bet for Arthur Ashe to win Wimbledon. This stunned Joey; he didn't think him capable of walking into a bookies let alone have the bottle to place a bet with that amount of money. His honesty defied belief. He told Joey that at a meeting before he came he confessed to the group that he wanked up to five times a day! Joey tried tactfully to explain that there were times it was best to keep schtum and there was a real danger of him pulling his pecker off. Over the coming months Joey became more and more aware of the frailties of his pitiful young ward mate.

John was a raving lunatic who only lasted on the unit a few days because he was a raving lunatic. Joey bumped into him every now and then when he started to go to occupational therapy but never spoke to him much.

Joey was a bit awkward with the girls. Having attended an all-boys school and drifting into the building game he wasn't used to their company. Not sober anyway. The girls he knew to date were usually met in the afterglow of a pint and a bag of pork scratchings. Even Christine who he'd seen on and off for four years never knew him outside the pub. In fact, from the age of nineteen his life had condensed more and more into a pint mug. Joey found himself enjoying the company of the girls, particularly Ann. He studied her sat in the lounge in the evenings trying to fathom what tormented her enough to completely mutilate her arms. There didn't seem to be an inch of unbroken skin the length of her forearms that didn't wield a scar. He remembered that poor woman in admission with the horrendous neck scar. Maybe he could kiss Ann's scars. What was this thing he had about kissing scars? What didn't she like about herself? He liked her. He fancied her.

Joey was pretty gloomy a couple of weeks later when told after the weekend that Ann would not be returning to the group. No details were given and he hadn't known her long enough to chase things up. He wasn't the chasing up sort anyway; a trait that pissed him off more and more as he aged. He got on well with the other girls except Sam who irritated him. A white Brummie girl who spoke half the time in Pidgin English, very often replying to the speaker with 'yous tarkin ta me honky?' Joey never asked or wanted to know why, he only knew it fuckin' irritated him.

Group therapy meetings were held every morning between 9 and 10. On Mondays and Wednesdays the shrink and hospital chaplain sat in along with the nursing staff. Most of the meetings finished with hardly a word spoken. Now and again the shrink, after spending 'alf-hour loading and lighting his pipe, would initiate conversation and occasionally this led to debate but not often or relevant enough for Joey to ever think he was gonna get over whatever it was he needed to get over to get out of there and live a normal life.

Jake would spark things up now and again with his banal comments and disrespect for anything or body. Lyn, an articulate black girl not long with the group sussed Jake out straight off and wound him up so tight that the inevitable 'shut the fuck up you black bastard' generally ended the meet early. Joey could see by the wry smile on Lyn's face that she had enjoyed putting up Jake's pea-brain in a glass case for the museum of neo-Nazi memorabilia.

Adam spent every meeting staring at the floor and picking his thumbs. He picked at them so much that large wart-like appendages grew on his thumb joints. Joey was going nowhere. What was supposed to be happening? Who was gonna make him better? Why had that 'Doctor' laid into him?

The nursing staff on the unit were more approachable than in admission, although they spent a lot of time tucked away in a small office. All except Staff Nurse George, who seemed to go out of his way to embrace the ethos of the unit. 'Black as a cat' his mother reckoned. He was certainly that and he knew his mother's simile to be one of endearment because she loved cats. Joey's mother was born and raised in Aston and remembered when she was young the influx of immigrants to the inner city areas. She often spoke of the times people would leave the house if a black man or woman walked down the road because they'd never seen one in the flesh. So Staff Nurse George being as 'black as a cat' to his mother was okay. Staff Nurse George was of Nigerian descent and however black he was as compared to a cat he lit up Joey's path like a street lamp. A deep thinker, his hand often wrapped round his chin and his brow furrowed in concentration, he listened, gave advice but best of all offered sincerity which Joey picked up on. Joey liked to make him laugh, to set him off howling in typical afro-Caribbean style - white toothed and raucous. Joey found his laugh infectious and looked forward to his shifts.

Later, at the funeral, Staff Nurse George showed his worth as a man and saint.

Apart from the company of George, Joey just wasn't getting what was going on. The meetings became as much use to him as a kick in the bollocks and after months on the unit he was scared for his future.

He started to study the shrink smoking his pipe. Could he blow smoke rings? Even better could he blow smoke bubbles? Maybe he could puff a smoke bubble inside his head with him in it to have a look around. Yeah, that's it; he could puff a big bubble for him then puff smaller bubbles inside the big bubble for his nursing staff and the smaller bubbles could orbit round inside the bigger bubble. A solar system of smokey bubbles. Maybe he could puff a biggish bubble, a bit smaller than the bigger bubble but bigger than the smaller bubbles for thousand bricks a day man. No! He wouldn't see through the psychotic smoke - he just didn't get neurotic - like a dyslexia cynic-bad parenting. He'd pop the bubbles.

Bubble pop

    lubbop bop

       popple bub

        pup blebbo

        pleb obubb

lebbop bulp.

He'd hooked up with his mates again going home for weekends and was drinking as heavily as ever. His anxiety levels had gone through the roof, as had his consumption levels of alcohol and the problem of facing up to the world without substance abuse was even more apparent than when he admitted himself to hospital. He felt isolated in his misery; he could neither explain nor understand what was going on and suicidal ideation began to stalk him again. He had no idea where he fitted in the diagnostic jigsaw of mental health. Neurotic, psychotic; it all meant the same to him - we're all fuckin' barmy! He'd started to miss the Monday morning meetings because he stank of the drink needed to take the bus.

Staff Nurse George had suggested to Joey that occupational therapy might be of some help to him; break the day up a bit, keep his mind engaged. A couple of mornings he'd go to the art department where he rediscovered his artistic flair that had been in evidence at junior school level - the only thing he discovered at senior level was how brutal grown men could be - the head master being a former borstal head who took his de-humanistic approach to comprehensive level.

On other days he'd sit in a workshop wiring up lampshades. He sat at the end of the table checking that the shades had been wired correctly; him being relatively un-insane he got the important job. Here he met Roy. He was a little older than Joey and very peculiar looking. His tightly curled hair to the sides of his head stuck out like a couple of glued on shredded wheat while the top of his head lacked the same profusion of hair giving a look of the red sea parting for Moses. The poor sod had nothing going for him physically. Bulbous eyes protruded like someone had hold of his knackers and his huge beak started its sweep at the bridge of the nose almost hooking round on itself at lip level.

He introduced himself to Joey by telling him that he worked in the reptile house at Dudley Zoo and had had a mental breakdown. Two things struck Joey; one of puzzlement - what the fuck's the difference between a mental breakdown and a nervous one? He'd been in the place for over 6 months and he still knew fuck-all about mental health terminology. The second was one of wonderment - did Dudley Zoo know yet they were missing a 6 foot chameleon?

Joey was hopelessly depressed again. He'd put himself into the care of people who he thought would put him right but had gained a level of nihilism that both pissed him off or amused him depending on sky colour. He knew he was on his own and faced a lifetime of struggle in which he would have to find a way of dealing with or become scar ridden at each failed attempt.

After one particularly drunken weekend he shook into OT. Feeling like his skin was on inside out making him raw edged, jumpy and paranoid. He wanted no contact or communication. He sat opposite Roy feeling like a bag of shite. Trembling, choking back tears; 24 years old now and feeling like 24 years was just about enough - he didn't feel greedy for any more. He placed his hand rolling baccy and zippo lighter on the table in front of him and began to watch Roy. He couldn't shake the metaphor that Roy represented mankind's belly crawl onto dry land when all he wanted to do was crawl back into the mire where it all began. He freaked out when Roy's four foot long sticky tongue started flicking out snatching items from the table. He pocketed his lighter. He just wasn't up for rolling round the floor wrestling a giant chameleon for ownership of a zippo. He had to get out of there!

Joey was woken one night by a member of staff who asked him if he would help them out. Adam had climbed forty foot up a huge water tower in the hospital grounds and was threatening to jump if they didn't fetch Joey. Joey dressed and followed. At the tower a police car was parked up and quite a number of hospital staff. Someone shouted up to Adam that Joey was there.

'Tell them Joey!'

'Tell them I'll jump!'

'They don't believe me! Tell them I will Joey!'

Adam's voice was so pitiful that it lumped up Joey's throat.

'It's ok Adam, I'm here, come down mate.'

Joey felt hopeless. The self-conscious bell-rope that was ruining his life strangled him into silence.

'Tell them I'll do it Joey!'

A sudden surge of bravery sent Joey towards the steps of the water tower but he was stopped from going up by staff members. Cold and emotion made him tremble. He couldn't see the top of the tower but he knew that Adam might jump; he had always known that Adam might jump, even when he'd heard staff members mock between themselves that he was just a poor little rich kid needing attention. Why could only he see it? Adam continued to wail; Joey put his hand over his ears - for fucks sake help the kid! Joey visualised Adam falling from the skies and backed himself under the safety of a nearby Sycamore tree – this upset him so much that he couldn't sleep that night.

After God-only knows how long he could hear footsteps on the checker plate steps. Adam was led down by a policeman who he hadn't known was up there. He had a blanket wrapped round his head and shoulders. They looked at each other. Adam had the heart-rending look of a frightened waif peering through the cloak of the ghost of Christmas yet to be. They placed him gently into the police car.

This was the last time Joey was to see him alive.

After returning to the unit from another weekend Staff Nurse George told Joey that Adam had taken his own life. He'd hosed up his smart car and choked himself.

At the funeral Joey was so shaken up with nervous emotion that he could barely stand. Staff Nurse George put his arm round him to steady him up. A typical gesture from a rare man; a man that Joey lost contact with and never forgave himself for.

As Joey stood waiting with his cases for a lift home after discharging himself with the promise of being an out-patient - which he did for a few weeks before drifting off, back into the darkness - he pondered over what had happened and what he'd learnt. Would he be back in there? Probably because he felt fuck-all different to when he went in. No! He was worse. He was now pretty much certain that he was on his own with this thing and his life would be spent digging deep into resources that others tapped into only in times of crisis; not for getting out of bed in the morning. The human resources that made up the hospital staff had turned a sick man into a cripple. Why should a young man who crushed his body for a living have his mind crushed by a chancer not fit to make a living. Why should he watch another blow smoke bubbles from a pipe in a room where the young gasp for freedom and clarity? Eight months and he now remembers the name of one nurse. Oh, and the young mutilate their beautiful bodies - or end their existence by way of their own, delicate, gentle hands.

Big Gerry had been in touch - was he ready to load up for another lift? Up to scaffold height.

In the store Joey had traipsed his way round behind his wife to the check-out point. The moths had fallen silent and lined up along the cable trays pulsating light with heartbeat. Joey thought they were watching him; one moth was shifting position, trying to re-balance with a gentle wing-flutter. What was it saying? He turned back round to face his wife and saw the vulnerability of the world in the back of her small head. Two hairs had dislodged themselves onto the back of her fleece which nearly bought him to his knees. *Let me go woman, let go of me.* After clearing out her purse Joey helped his wife load up the shopping into cardboard boxes. He brushed past her towards the door.

'Please; don't go out there,' she said.

He looked through the glass frontage of the store. There was nothing there; no people, cars; just a fine grey mist like ashen fallout from a far-away eruption. In the distance tiny bobs of light, like fireflies disappeared one by one into the haze.

'But I want to go.'

'No - not yet; it's not your time.'

'Why?'

'Because we'd miss you too much; and I love you.'

He studied her face as he took in the simple statement; she looked young again, glorious.

'But I saw the Great Moths.'

'I know you did; but they've gone now.'

Joey looked round the store and they had gone, without a trace. The place was as it once was and how it should always be. He turned to face his wife again and she smiled. Joey returned the smile because Joey always returned smiles. She passed him the trolley.

'You carry the load; I'll foot the ladders.'

Hammerite Spider

Resolution

For Jack
A.m. - New Year's Day.

Limping a wet track
Sodden through, slipshod
With two companions:
A dog with a bad ear and
A child with a half blocked flue.

The dog on ahead for a head whistle
Turns, cocks its head siff curious
Wax maddened, wagging.
The child, puffing, whispering
Trying to structure a breathing pattern
Stops; picks coloured stones
From the field's edge.
Volumatic breath struggles, but blows
Straw from kaleidoscopic rock
And, discovering new colours,
Pockets them…

This dog is gonna still refuse
Not to hear tunes, through a deaf ear
From the dead

Mud.

Atonement

I remember your tender hands trembled

When I had you by the throat.

Chokin' – I see them now

Smokin' – I choke some more.

I want to cross the park to that hoodie with his mad
mongrel staff

And knock him out – let the crazed dog savage me.

Redemption of the hitman

When his gangster's gone to church

        Forsaking

The free peanuts and an 'arf-ten lurch

She has psalms in her eyes.

Takes wine with Mary and toasts

The ghosts of poverty in a different way.

When her gangster sheaves his stiletto

And kneels at the feet of a glorious mother

Who takes his frail head in her frail hands

        Sanctifying

His weakness in a halo of sweetness

She has tears in her eyes - love's leaking proof

For a spirit disarmed.

Return to Blackpool

It's amazing how, on ring-o-bells day

A hover mower with heave and grunt

Will spin and blitz pegs, slugs, doggy dumps.

A traversing cursing wreck, tadpole friend

Who now likes to swim with the newts

Must change his kegs for Sunday suits,

And a tie of course to fool the pull

In his eyes, red waxen face, check pence

Commence the liqueur race.

Strange poignancy for a winner who

Shakes down the street with an armpit sweat

Crossing the road for a fear of being met.

My round your round my round your.....

Spirit upended, straight backed eased eye

Malt befriended - solace gained

From a return ticket to Blackpool.

Hammerite spider

My runny nose -

Everywhere but on its dewdrop

The twilight fades.

It had taken two days for his face to cool down after his latest bender. On the third morning he woke early - too early - he knew the signs. He drew his arm up through the sheets and felt his forehead; he could have fried an egg on it a few days before but now the furnace was out and the cremated remains of his self-esteem, skull trapped, smouldered in the nothingness. He closed his eyes in shame. *What happens to me?* A couple of weeks ago he was buzzing. He remembered lying in the same bed trying to sleep. There was no shame then though - just dancing eyeballs. Back then every time he shut his eyes he visualised standing in the mouth of a vast moonlit cavern emptying itself of tens of thousands of bats. He felt the wing flapped air, heard the cacophony of deranged flight and from within saw the fire lit by the last Neanderthal that spooked them into flight. He remembered the brightness of the moon, like a buttered cracker, and every time a frenzied bat flapped across the moon his closed eyes followed, darting from side to side up and down faster than a pumped up South America footballer crossing himself. It drove him fuckin' mad! He had to keep getting out of bed - tele on-tele off, fag, walk in the 3 o'clock-in-the-morning garden until exhaustion finally flaked him out.

Now he stood in the black silent cavern alone; just him and the reek of a million crapped out moths. He was sinking fast, sinking deep – and he knew it.

He thought about her eyes; the woman lying back to back with him in bed, just seventeen when she met him. Her eyes attracted him then; the whites of her eyes, daisy white, naive; eyes that had never looked further than out to sea from a caravan window on the south coast on holiday with her parents. Both her parents were dead now – all she had left in her life were her beautiful children and a fuckin' lunatic.

The woman in his life: loved – hated; treated with dignity – vilified; whispered softly to; growled at. In the quiet room he sensed her presence but wasn't certain that she was there. She'd done a runner the week before to her friend's house and only returned the previous day – or did she? She knew the signs as well – long before he did. He inched his foot back slowly to check; as their ankles met she drew her foot away. The first light began to show itself through a gap in the curtains. The calendar said something about it being spring. He heard a bird sing – he liked birds.

He didn't lie there too long. His lungs started to poke him to get up and take his first fag. He crept down the stairs trying hard not to wake the kids. His legs had jellified. As he lowered himself to each tread they trembled with the weakness of not eating properly for weeks. Eating had got in the way of drinking. He couldn't have that. But now he'd crashed the physical need for sustenance just wasn't there. His mind had rejected his body.

In the kitchen he put the kettle on and went outside under the lean-to to roll his ciggie. He struggled to roll a decent fag. His hands had stopped shaking but his forefingers and thumbs still twitched involuntarily. The finished fag looked like a limp dick but it would have to do. He lit up and drew heavily through clenched teeth. After his fix he went back into the kitchen to make a brew. He had similar problems with the tea making. Even the short distance from the sugar caddie to the mug resulted in sugar being spilt all over the worktop and the tiled floor. *What a fucking mess!*

He peered out through the kitchen window into the dimly lit garden. Scattered across the garden were dozens of dwarf conifers and heathers still in their pots. Half had been blown over by the spring winds. In the far corner of the garden was a pile of red sandstone rocks. *Tell me then, tell me.*

He cast his mind back to a few weeks previous and recalled how he'd suddenly decided that he was a better gardener than Alan Titchmarsh, so he nagged and persuaded his wife to take him to Norfolk after reading in some sort of gardening mag that there was a 'specialist' nursery offering 'specially selected' conifers and heathers at competitive prices just for your garden. She kept insisting that the garden centre 2 miles down the road offered the same plants at the same prices, but his mind was fixated with Norfolk. So Norfolk was where they had to go; a 350 mile round trip. Although she knew the financial madness of it all, his wife secretly enjoyed it when her husband was rockin' and rollin'; she felt part of him, felt that he really needed her - she knew it wouldn't last though. So there they were; on the way back from Norfolk with half the mortgage money bedded in various sized pots crammed out in the back of their battered old Ford Estate; he even had half a dozen on his lap in the passenger seat.

The red sandstone was next. He vaguely remembered going on a fishing trip with his mate some years earlier and travelling along a road near a town called Bewdley. He recalled how the road cut through a section of sandstone cliff and how, over the years, rocks had dislodged themselves and lay scattered along the roadside. *Yes! Red sandstone for the rockery!* He hired a tranny van for this trip and decided to take the kids for company.

He had to really battle against the urges to drive flat out and endanger his beloved children. It was pissing down; he did find the place though and parked up half on the busy road and half on the grass bank. The kids were young; young enough not to feel embarrassed watching their old man, soaked to the skin, slipping and sliding about on the hillside gathering rocks. They thought it was hilarious, particularly when he spotted a stone that he just had to have halfway up the steepest section of the hillside. The kids cracked up as he came skidding down the hill on his arse with a massive rock on his lap. So there he was again; dripping wet, a ton of sandstone in the back of the tranny, on his way home singing 'Old McDonald' to the kids at the top of his voice. Something started to go wrong that night. His wife didn't seem to share his enthusiasm, he started to feel irritable.

After making another brew he took his tea and baccy out into the brick built shed. He felt he belonged in a shed, it suited his moods. When he was buzzing it became his drinking den. He liked to smoke himself silly and set out along the liquor road before the pub crawl, sometimes as early as 7 am. He usually started with diamond whites – nice taste – if he went straight for the vodka he would probably retch so the diamond whites became his starter, his prawn cocktail before the maniacal mayhem of the day. When his body and mindset was nailed he went for the vodka and by opening time he was ready.

He'd moved from the city some years ago and he preferred the pubs there. He could trawl from pub to pub without much fuss and after several days he'd usually end up in one of the get-the-fuck-outta-here places that exist on most housing estates. He liked the risk, the threat of bother, of violence; strange for a man who detested violence.

In a village life was different, he had to be smarter. He had to visit the couple of more respectable, food orientated pubs first before he got larier and started to stagger. People knew him in the village, they knew when he was out of character, this niggled him. There wasn't the twisted anonominity like the estates, he had to use his head here, plan it out, plan the binge properly. That was the theory anyway; it all went out of the window later in the day, he got it wrong last time and he ended up in a smarter real ale type of place. The piss artists still existed in them but they were able to hide it behind the respectability of supping real ale. He remembers reading some of the daft names of the ale – Boondoggle – Hooters Trough – Speckled Hen – they asked him to leave when he called out for a pint of Squashed Hedgehog.

He recalled the last session on Sunday night when the blaming of others gave way to a tearful sadness. When the landlord helped him home.

He sat down on an old tool chest in the shed; the aura had changed in there now. It no longer tempted him to drink, although he could still smell alcohol along with the faint whiff of wood preserver that he had knocked over when he was tempted to taste it some days ago. *Why preserve wood – why preserve any fuckin' thing!* Now the haven of the shed became the personification of gloom. An elevated sadness overwhelmed him. He could suddenly sense the creatures he was sharing the room with. He knew of the battles taking place all around him in the dank, manky atmosphere. Spidery lairs, sudden deathly movements in the dark corners of walls, amongst the piles of discarded junk, old furniture, rusted nail boxes, off cuts of timber turned grey in the must. He stared into abandoned silks at the remnants of life; looking for clues, for colour: a crane fly leg, a moths head with one wing still attached, bits of what looked like a ladybird - *fuck* - he liked ladybirds. There was some strange affiliation taking place between a mind flailing in its own webs of degeneracy and the inside of a man - made shell fit for life frenetic, half eaten away and the arachnoid screams.

He rolled another fag and drew heavily. He knew he might be on borrowed time after the dentist had spotted a white patch under his tongue and sent him to the maxi-facial clinic for a biopsy. A week later a young Scottish doctor told him there were changes taking place and he had to pack up smoking. He mumbled a lie telling him that he had cut down but the doctor wasn't listening – you have to stop smoking – you have to stop smoking.

He drew heavily again concentrating the smoke under his tongue. As he watched the blue smoke swirling in the sunlight that was now illuminating the window something caught his eye on the shed floor. He reached down and picked up a dead robin. The bird was still fairly supple which told him that it couldn't have been dead long. *How did it die? How can something that looks so sublime in death die so young? It doesn't look old enough to die – no, it can't be. I must have killed it somehow – did I poison it with my breath*? He studied the bird and saw God. He saw God holding his creation in cupped hands, and as the first flecks of snow descended to the earth he puffed the bird into the white world to sing and show itself to all those who were struggling to see it through to the spring.

His own hands felt brutal as he held the bird. He placed it into his left hand and used the back of the forefinger of his right hand to stroke its chest. He barely wanted to lay his finger on the bird, he wanted to stroke it with the merest of touches but it was hopeless. His twitching finger wasn't having any of it. He was making a right mess of its plumage. The perfection of the dead bird was lost; its feathers now bedraggled. The bird now looked dead. *No not like that! Stroke the fucking thing properly*! He placed the bird onto the tool chest beside him and sunk his elbows into his knees. Tears welled in his eyes as he stared at the floor of the shed. As he wiped the snot from his nose a teardrop dripped onto the inside of his specs. He took them off to clean and saw the blurred shape of a rusted carpenters axe propped up in the corner of the shed. He had an urge to chop his finger off.

After an age in the shed smoking and drinking tea his wife opened the door and told him that Chris the fish had rung and asked if he was going over today to do the work he'd promised to do. She reminded him that they had no money and that he really needed to do the work. 'Okay' was the only response he could muster.

Chris the fish was a market trader; a fishmonger who'd inherited a big, vastly extended old farmhouse just across the road from him. The place was set in about 3 acres of land and over the last few years he'd worked for him nearly every

Saturday, cash in hand because the place was in need of quite major refurbishment. Very often this was the only money available to feed the family through the week. He liked Chris the fish; they got on well and he'd supplied him with regular work and never failed to pay him. His wife was a doctor of science, a strange mix but he liked her as well.

He eventually managed to stir into some sort of action. He threw the tools he thought he'd need into one of his toolboxes. A carpenter by trade, a good one a times but the quality of his work tended to go up and down with his moods. He could turn his hand to most building trades and had, when he was right, a reputation of being a good all round tradesman. He took a look at the dead robin, he'd bury it later, on another day he might just fuck it in the bin.

To get to Chris the fish's house he had to cross a shared bridge over a brook and he often stopped to stare into the water. He liked to look at the sticklebacks in the shallow water. Fuck knows why. This morning the sun was bright and just high enough to cast shadows of the fish – *in the shadows of sticklebacks* – he liked that – he liked sticklebacks. He was low. He was pretty sure by now that he was heading for a major. As he stared at the fish he thought how easy it would be to lie face down in the shallow water and let the sticklebacks cast their shadows onto his lifeless fingers.

He managed to drag himself away from the bridge and made his way to Chris the fish's house. He'd been there many times to do a variety of jobs to the house, outbuildings and garden. They trusted him enough to give him a key to the place. The fish and his wife had already left for work but he knew the schedule of work for the day – renovate an old cast iron garden bench, re-felt the gazebo roof and make a start scraping and preparing the timber sash windows ready for painting. He really didn't want to do anything but something kept him going. Whether it was the money he desperately needed or an inherent personality trait that didn't want to let people down he couldn't tell, but he really didn't want to do anything but find a secluded spot in the garden and stare into space. He had to work; he decided to tackle the garden bench first. This was a heavy piece of kit with ornate cast iron ends and back slatted with good quality hardwood. He didn't want to move it far because he couldn't be arsed so he rummaged through the old stables and found a thin 8x4 sheet of plywood that was no good for any kind of structural work. The glue in the veneers had broken down but it would be ideal for placing underneath the bench to catch the drips of paint and protect the slabbed area where the bench was sited next to the border of the garden. The first attempt to lift the bench onto the plywood resulted in him dropping one of the feet onto his toes. After a round of 'fucks' he tried again, and managed to position the bench so that he could work in some sort of reasonable fashion. The bench itself was in pretty poor condition. The protective cover was peeling off the cast iron and rust was showing through the flaking areas. Chris the fish had left a can of black hammerite, some emery cloth and a new brush to tackle the job. He made a poor job of the preparation. Everything was now a major effort. He hacked off the main areas of flaking paint but couldn't be bothered to sand it back and feather the joins between sound paintwork and bare iron. He couldn't even muster enough will to dust it down and remove the cobwebs, bits of decayed leaf and debris that had lodged itself into the ornate ironwork. He should really have laid the bench on its back and scrubbed it down thoroughly but his mental strength had sapped away and everything now was a major ball ache.

He opened the can of hammerite with a screwdriver and gave it a few stirs with a length of dirty bamboo that he'd picked up in the vegetable patch – *fuck it – I'll just paint over the cobwebs and shit and see what it looks like.* He lay down resting his left elbow on the plywood, loaded his brush with the hammerite and started to paint underneath the bench where the timber slats were bolted through. The sun was bright in his eyes but it was early spring and the cold blow felt sharp on his hands and face. He was going through the motions; he'd painted a thousand things before so he needed little concentration, not that he could think straight anyway.

He loaded his brush again and stabbed it up into the corner of the cast iron. Something plopped onto the plywood. He looked down and to his horror it started to move. It was a spider! Perfectly coated with black hammerite. Not just a spider but a fat bellied garden spider – he liked fat bellied garden spiders – as a kid he used to stun flies and other creepy crawlies and flick them into the webs and watch as the spider moved in for the kill. He used to search for the biggest ones and was always amazed at the brilliant colours on their little round bodies. Now here he was staring at one coated in black hammerite. He watched in disbelief as the spider inched its way across the plywood – *fuck me! It's leaving footprints! Spider prints!* He was mesmerised. The spider was painted to perfection – *how could that be?* It was as if it had been painted by an ancient Chinese master. There were no runs anywhere on its painted body. Its legs looked as if they had been picked out with the tiniest brush in the hands of a genius. Tears began to well as he watched the spider stumbling its way across the plywood towards the border of the garden. *What's it doing? Why is it battling to survive? Why doesn't it just curl up and die plunged into a world of chemicals? What will happen to it when the hammerite cures? A shell of hammerite in the shape of a spider like some sort of ancient artifact taken from an Egyptian tomb. What about when the spider starts to shrivel up inside the set casing – what will the chemical compound created in the gap between the shriveling spider and the hammerite be? Spidergen – Hammer oxide – there'll be some sort of new gas in the gap. What gap! What gas! What fucking gap! What are you thinking about you barmy bastard!* Tears were streaming down his face now as the spider stumbled off the plywood onto the earth of the garden border. He began to sob. The spider somehow managed to upend itself onto its feet but the hammerite had picked up some little specks of dirt which spoiled the paintwork – *fuck it!* Desperate, he started to paint over the spider prints. He wanted his wife to come over and tell him it was alright; that he'd never wanted it to happen, that it wasn't his fault. He didn't want to die. He needed someone to explain. He took one last look at the spider disappearing between the heathers and the bluebell shoots – struggling to live – not ready to die.

Don't leave

Don't leave me blossom when the colours fade

You looked so good in orange, that night

Still light at ten; in the garden, in the heart.

When the cold blow rattles the leaves and me

Way beyond your reasoning; come after us,

On the bus, to the wards; we need you.

Don't leave me blossom now the colour's faded

You look so good in orange.

Haiku for Issa

Walking the woods

With his daughter

He heard the elves whispering.

Butterfly

Get out the wind!

Your knickers are showing.

Take a maggot

Winter robin

The fish aren't biting.

Fruitless analogy with the task of trying to fathom anxiety

We spooked a shoal of golden chub

With our warm, meaning no harm

Surface shadow. He asked what frightened them.

I jumbled something about ground vibrations

Predators, fear of human contact.

But what I really wanted to say was:

My little friend; I have as much idea

What fears

Those fins that fan

From tree root safety, to mouth muted complexities

As the poetic pebbles that shimmer, half hidden

Beneath their wavering shadows.

Care-plan: bi-polar disorder - 'currently euthymic'

If I; soul worn; shook off me dancing boots

And trawled bare-foot on rain forest paths

Where one foot, wrongly stepped, could be

Toxin-fanged. Or longed for the silent pipe blown

Frog-tipped-dart of death: I could sit there; fucked;

Tree backed, legs outstretched with me pants full

Of ants and watch: as the hooped bands slither away

The twigs show legs and sway; echo

The gathering monkeys' howl.

Dueling thought strings

As the honest priest shapes
His words to suit the needs
Of the gathered few and
For the deliverance of
A too young boy in a lacquered
Box who stumbled and fell
I pluck the banjoed notes
From a suggestive word
                           Pa-pa-pam   pam   par.
As I turn to the side and see
The sad sunken eyes of
The Grandmother to the boy
In the box too young for this
I see a weird eyed boy on
A river straddled bridge with
His musical piece swinging
To and fro and strum the
Guitars reply
                           Der-der-dum   dum   dar.
As the cask rolls in with
The boxed up boy too
Young to die I curse a
Mind like mine that can
Be flippant and find
These sad sick tunes
That drum up out of the blue.

Inner city dimples

On his knees chin-deep the boatman braved

A gentle flow; and took to the fringes - rainbowed.

Where no grub, emergent wing or things that sting

Affect his way.

A dapper-dude-dipping in the junk

Slick water punter bobbing about dead

Fish (he knows the market well; knows

Where the water's warmest).

As does the damsel queen who watches:

An emerald sari-swathed smooth jewel

From a rough cut.

Wind flickering - her silken veil;

Her perfect wings

     Smiling

         Dimple-daft.

Safe hands

For P.B.

For forty years I've felt in safe hands with you.

Through all the drunken mayhem, the bleak despair.

On your hospital visit I felt in safer hands with you

Than I did the nurses.

I light and pass you a ciggie.

And even though arthritis has shook you by the hands

And you've lost your grip - you've never lost your grip

If you know what I mean. And anyhow -

I still feel as if I'm in safe hands.

Old gravel workings

There must be love here; there has to be
Between these wooded aisles of paths and pools.
Worked out once for one resource, filled with
another
By men whose bones now lie as deep as these.

There must be peace here; now these self-inflicted
scars
Have calmly healed; deep plumptious-blue like
polished
Slate. Even the cormorants hang their heads in
shame
Driven inland from fish-depleted shores.

Don't bring the hammer down; not here; not now
No need to crucify mankind's gilded flaws
Where peace meets quiet, bush meets bream and
Willows sip the waters, ladylike, through leafy
straws.

There must be hope here; there has to be
For these once gaping wounds to have so
Beautifully healed.

Tangified

For Judith

Now the last ripples of a troubled mind
Have waved out and melted, and through forgiving
Mists we meet again on the car park of this man-
made lake.
Early morning, in the ninth month, after months
apart
Me living like an exiled hermit in a lonely bedsit
Drinking Stella, watching crane flies bounce
Off the glass under a half-cut moon; you lonely
And afraid in our once shared home.

We walk awhile in silence, I hold your hand, am
grateful
That I am not dead; the sun breaks through the
mist
As the mallards follow in the hope of bread.
The sorrow in your face upsets me, eyes tinged
pink
With so many tears; I hold you close to kiss
Your hair, hand and golden rings - mouth a prayer -
Lord release us from these manic swings.

Hammerite Spider